Slog's
dad

Slog's dad

David Almond

illustrated by

Dave McKean

WALKER
BOOKS

For Paul and Anne Mack

D. A.

This one's for my dad, Fred —
who never came back;
unless you count his
daily visits via my genes
through my hand,
onto the page.

D. M.

Spring had come. I'd been running round all day with Slog and we were starving. We were crossing the square to Myers' pork shop. Slog stopped dead in his tracks.

"What's up?" I said.

He nodded across the square.

"Look," he said.

"Look at what?"

"It's me dad," he whispered.

"Your dad?"

"Aye."

I just looked at him.

"That bloke there," he said.

"What bloke where?"

"Him on the bench. Him with the cap on. Him with the stick."

I shielded my eyes from the sun with my hand and tried to see. The bloke had his hands resting on the top of the stick. He had his chin resting on his hands. His hair was long and tangled and his clothes were tattered and worn, like he was poor or like he'd been on a long journey. His face was in the shadow of the brim of his cap, but you could see that he was smiling.

"Slogger, man," I said. "Your dad's dead."

"I know that, Davie. But it's him. He's come back again, like he said he would. In the spring."

He raised his arm and waved.

"Dad!" he shouted. "Dad!"

The bloke waved back.

"See?" said Slog. "Howay."

He tugged my arm.

"No," I whispered. "No!"

And I yanked myself free and I went into Myers', and Slog ran across the square to his dad.

Slog's dad had been a binman, a skinny bloke with a creased face and a greasy flat cap. He was always puffing on a Woodbine. He hung on to the back of the bin wagon as it lurched through the estate, jumped off and on, slung the bins over his shoulder, tipped the muck into the back. He was forever singing hymns – "Faith of Our Fathers", "Hail Glorious Saint Patrick", stuff like that.

"Here he comes again," my mam would say as he bashed the bins and belted out "Oh, Sacred Heart" at eight o'clock on a Thursday morning.

But she'd be smiling, because everybody liked Slog's dad, Joe Mickley, a daft and canny soul.

First sign of his illness was just a bit of a limp: then Slog came to school one day and said, "Me dad's got a black spot on his big toenail."

"Just like *Treasure Island*, eh?" I said.

"What's it mean?" he said.

I was going to say death and doom, but I said, "He could try asking the doctor."

"He has asked the doctor."

Slog looked down. I could smell his dad on him, the scent of rotten rubbish that was always on him. They lived just down the street from us, and the whole house had that smell in it, no matter how much Mrs Mickley washed and scrubbed. Slog's dad knew it. He said it was the smell of the earth. He said there'd be nowt like it in Heaven.

"The doctor said it's nowt," Slog said. "But he's staying in bed today, and he's going to hospital tomorrow. What's it mean, Davie?"

"How should I know?" I said.

I shrugged.

"It's just a spot, man, Slog!" I said.

Everything happened fast after that. They took the big toe off, then the foot, then the leg to halfway up the thigh. Slog said his mother reckoned his dad had caught some germs from the bins. My mother said it was all the Woodbines he puffed. Whatever it was, it seemed they stopped it. They fitted a tin leg on him and sent him home. It was the end of the bins, of course.

He took to sitting on the little garden wall outside the house. Mrs Mickley often sat with him and they'd be smelling their roses and nattering and smiling and swigging tea and puffing Woodbines. He used to show off his new leg to passers-by.

"I'll get the old one back when I'm in Heaven," he said.

If anybody asked was he looking for work, he'd laugh.

"Work? I can hardly bliddy walk."

And he'd start in on "Faith of Our Fathers" and everybody'd smile.

Then he got a black spot on his other big toenail, and they took him away again, and they started chopping at his other leg, and Slog said it was like living in a horror picture.

When Slog's dad came home next, he spent his days parked in a wheelchair in his garden. He didn't bother with tin legs: just pyjama bottoms folded over his stumps. He was quieter. He sat day after day in the summer sun among his roses, staring out at the pebble-dashed walls and the red roofs and the empty sky. The Woodbines dangled in his fingers, "Oh, Sacred Heart" drifted gently from his lips. Mrs Mickley brought him cups of tea, glasses of beer, Woodbines. Once I stood with Mam at the window and watched Mrs Mickley stroke her husband's head and gently kiss his cheek.

"She's telling him he's going to get better," said Mam.

We saw the smile growing on Joe Mickley's face.

"That's love," said Mam. "True love."

Slog's dad still joked and called out to anybody passing by.

"Walk?" he'd say. "Man, I cannot even bliddy hop."

"They can hack your body to a hundred bits," he'd say. "But they cannot hack your soul."

We saw him shrinking. Slog told me he'd heard his mother whispering about his dad's fingers coming off. He told me about Mrs Mickley lifting his dad from the chair each night, laying him down, whispering her goodnights, like he was a little bairn. Slog said that some nights when he was really scared, he got into bed beside them.

"But it just makes it worse," he said. He cried. "I'm bigger than me dad, Davie. I'm bigger than me bliddy dad!"

And he put his arms around me and put his head on my shoulder and cried.

"Slog, man," I said as I tugged away. "Howay, Slogger, man!"

One day late in August, Slog's dad caught me looking. He waved me to him. I went to him slowly. He winked.

"It's alreet," he whispered. "I know you divent want to come too close."

He looked down to where his legs should be.

"They tell us if I get to Heaven I'll get them back again," he said. "What d'you think of that, Davie?"

I shrugged.

"Dunno, Mr Mickley," I said.

"Do you reckon I'll be able to walk back here if I do get them back again?"

"Dunno, Mr Mickley."

I started to back away.

"I'll walk straight out them pearly gates," he said. He laughed. "I'll follow the smells. There's no smells in Heaven. I'll follow the bliddy smells right back here to the lovely earth."

He looked at me.

"What d'you think of that?" he said.

Just a week later, the garden was empty. We saw Doctor Molly going in, then Father O'Mahoney, and just as dusk was coming on, Mr Blenkinsop, the undertaker.

The week after the funeral, I was heading out of the estate for school with Slog, and he told me, "Dad said he's coming back."

"Slogger, man," I said.

"His last words to me. Watch for me in the spring, he said."

"Slogger, man. It's just cos he was…"

"What?"

I gritted my teeth.

"Dying, man!"

I didn't mean to yell at him, but the traffic was thundering past us on the bypass. I got hold of his arm and we stopped.

"Bliddy dying," I said more softly.

"Me mam says that and all," said Slog. "She says we'll have to wait. But I cannot wait till I'm in Heaven, Davie. I want to see him here one more time."

Then he stared up at the sky.

"Dad," he whispered. "Dad!"

I got into Myers'. Chops and sausages and bacon and black pudding and joints and pies sat in neat piles in the window. A pink pig's head with its hair scorched off and a grin on its face gazed out at the square. There was a bucket of bones for dogs and a bucket of blood on the floor. The marble counters and Billy Myers' face were gleaming.

"Aye-aye, Davie," he said.

"Aye," I muttered.

"Saveloy, I suppose? With everything?"

"Aye. Aye."

I looked out over the pig's head. Slog was with the bloke, looking down at him, talking to him. I saw him lean down to touch the bloke.

"And a dip?" said Billy.

"Aye," I said.

He plunged the sandwich into a trough of gravy.

"Bliddy lovely," he said. "Though I say it myself.

A shilling to you, sir."

I paid him but I couldn't go out through the door. The sandwich was hot. The gravy was dripping to my feet.

Billy laughed.

"Penny for them," he said.

I watched Slog get onto the bench beside the bloke.

"Do you believe there's life after death?" I said.

Billy laughed.

"Now there's a question for a butcher!" he said.

A skinny old woman came in past me.

"What can I do you for, pet?" said Billy. "See you, Davie."

He laughed.

"Kids!" he said.

Slog looked that happy as I walked towards them. He was leaning on the bloke and the bloke was leaning back on the bench grinning at the sky. Slog made a fist and face of joy when he saw me.

"It's Dad, Davie!" he said. "See? I told you."

I stood in front of them.

"You remember Davie, Dad," said Slog.

The bloke looked at me. He looked nothing like the Joe Mickley I used to know. His face was filthy but it was smooth and his eyes were shining bright.

"Course I do," he said. "Nice to see you, son."

Slog laughed.

"Davie's a bit scared," he said.

"No wonder," said the bloke. "That looks very tasty."

I held the sandwich out to him.

He took it, opened it and smelt it and looked at the meat and pease pudding and stuffing and mustard and gravy. He closed his eyes and smiled, then lifted it to his mouth.

"Saveloy with everything," he said. He licked the gravy from his lips, wiped his chin with his hand. "Bliddy lovely. You got owt to drink?"

"No," I said.

"Ha. He has got a tongue!"

"He looks a bit different," said Slog. "But that's just cos he's been..."

"Transfigured," said the bloke.

"Aye," said Slog. "Transfigured. Can I show him your legs, Dad?"

The bloke laughed gently. He bit his saveloy sandwich. His eyes glittered as he watched me.

"Aye," he said. "Gan on. Show him me legs, son."

And Slog knelt at his feet and rolled the bloke's tattered trouser bottoms up and showed the bloke's dirty socks and dirty shins.

"See?" he whispered.

He touched the bloke's legs with his fingers.

"Aren't they lovely?" he said. "Touch them, Davie."

I didn't move.

"Gan on," said the bloke. "Touch them, Davie."

His voice got colder.

"Do it for Slogger, Davie," he said.

I crouched, I touched, I felt the hair and the skin and the bones and muscles underneath. I recoiled, I stood up again.

"It's true, see?" said Slog. "He got them back in Heaven."

"What d'you think of that, then, Davie?" said the bloke.

Slog smiled.

"He thinks they're bliddy lovely, Dad."

Slog stroked the bloke's legs one more time then rolled the trousers down again.

MEANWHILE...

MEANWHILE...

"What's Heaven like, Dad?" said Slog.

"Hard to describe, son."

"Please, Dad."

"It's like bright and peaceful and there's God and the angels and all that..." The bloke looked at his sandwich. "It's like having all the saveloy dips you ever want. With everything, every time."

"It must be great."

"Oh, aye, son. It's dead canny."

"Are you coming to see Mam, Dad?" he said.

The bloke pursed his lips and sucked in air and gazed into the sky.

"Dunno. Dunno if I've got the time, son."

Slog's face fell.

The bloke reached out and stroked Slog's cheek.

"This is very special," he said. "Very rare. They let it happen cos you're a very rare and special lad."

He looked into the sky and talked into the sky.

"How much longer have I got?" he said, then he nodded. "Aye. OK. OK."

He shrugged and looked back at Slog.

"No," he said. "Time's pressing. I cannot do it, son."

There were tears in Slog's eyes.

"She misses you that much, Dad," he said.

"Aye. I know." The bloke looked into the sky again. "How much longer?" he said.

He took Slog in his arms.

"Come here," he whispered.

I watched them hold each other tight.

"You can tell her about me," said the bloke. "You can tell her I love and miss her and all." He looked at me over Slog's shoulder. "And so can Davie, your best mate. Can't you, Davie? Can't you?"

"Aye," I muttered.

Across

1 Sorting and theft layman short
of a stand for (7,6)
7 I have bad habits, and incline to
crash (4)
8 Drunkenness at first trial (8)
9 Grass at the cape in the mud guest
10 Fire or thereabouts (6)
11 No time for (6)
12 Cash, nobody had in, in the
middle of — (6)
14 Slipper under the weather, you
make ratherness (5,7)
17 Having seen fast I great gate (12)
19 — (5)
20 Reason (3,3)
21 Money (3,3)
22 Also get signals making
errors on last image (8)

Down

2 Partially, require nothing but
of church (4)
3 Raise player has seen (3)
4 Conveyance or game (3)
5 Working cotton fabric aboard —
ship (5)
6 Insertion (7)
7 Fortification in Northern Ireland
(5)
13 Don't concern yourself with
Edward, the rat catcher (5,4)
15 Master destroyed, harassed
some owners (6)
16 Aluminium column seat —
arus private (8)
18 Make, dotage, Roger and
came (3)
21 Various patterns appear in part
of church (8)
24 Raise player has seen (3)
26 Inconvenience at first trial (4)

Britain's First

[article text too faded to read]

extraordi...
has been donat... man who disapp
refuse collector turned up alive at
after his Nationa... es, 57, who was th...
his widow Mary accident in the No...
olice station and c...
who has died age...t had no memory
...ry to piece togeth
...range Pyfe, Anne, who the...
as a slave-driver

e nothing but ...

...n game (3)
...fabric shrunk

...rthern Ireland

...urself with ...

	19			
20	I			
	N			22
	M			
25 M	A	R	Y	
	N			

Then the bloke stood up. Slog still clung to him.

"Can I come with you, Dad?" he said.

The bloke smiled.

"You know you can't, son."

"What did you do?" I said.

"Eh?" said the bloke.

"What job did you do?"

The bloke looked at me, dead cold.

"I was a binman, Davie," he said. "I used to stink but I didn't mind. And I followed the stink to get me here."

He cupped Slog's face in his hands.

"Isn't that right, son?"

"Aye," said Slog.

"So what's Slog's mother called?" I said.

"Eh?"

"Your wife. What's her name?"

The bloke looked at me. He looked at Slog. He pushed the last bit of sandwich into his mouth and chewed. A sparrow hopped close to our feet, trying to get at the crumbs. The bloke licked his lips, wiped his chin, stared into the sky.

"Please, Dad," whispered Slog.

The bloke shrugged. He gritted his teeth and sighed and looked at me so cold and at Slog so gentle.

"Slog's mother," he said. "My wife..." He shrugged again. "She's called Mary."

"Oh, Dad!" said Slog and his face was transfigured by joy. "Oh, Dad!"

The bloke laughed.

"Ha! Bliddy ha!"

He held Slog by the shoulders.

"Now, son," he said. "You got to stand here and watch me go and you mustn't follow."

"I won't, Dad," whispered Slog.

"And you must always remember me."

"I will, Dad."

"And me, you and your lovely mam'll be together again one day in Heaven."

"I know that, Dad. I love you, Dad."

"And I love you."

And the bloke kissed Slog, and twisted his face at me, then turned away. He started singing "Faith of Our Fathers". He walked across the square past Myers' pork shop, and turned down onto the High Street. We ran after him then and we looked down the High Street past the people and the cars but there was no sign of him, and there never would be again.

We stood there speechless. Billy Myers came to the doorway of the pork shop with a bucket of bones in his hand and watched us.

"That was me dad," said Slog.

"Aye?" said Billy.

"Aye. He come back, like he said he would, in the spring."

"That's good," said Billy. "Come and have a dip, son. With everything."

Slog's Dad was first commissioned as a short story by New Writing North and published in **So What Kept You?** (Flambard Press, 2006); then was runner-up in the 2007 National Short Story Prize, which led to its being published in **The National Short Story Prize** anthology (Atlantic Books, 2007), in **Prospect** magazine, and broadcast on BBC Radio 4.

First published 2010 by Walker Books Ltd

87 Vauxhall Walk, London SE11 5HJ

2 4 6 8 10 9 7 5 3 1

Text © 2006 David Almond

Illustrations © 2010 Dave M^CKean

The right of David Almond and Dave M^CKean to be identified as author and illustrator respectively of this work has been asserted by them in accordance with the Copyright, Designs and Patents Act 1988

This book has been typeset in Priori Sans

Printed in China

British Library Cataloguing in Publication Data: a catalogue record for this book is available from the British Library

ISBN 978-1-4063-2290-3

www.walker.co.uk